# VALI

THE VERY OCEANS AND MOUNTAINS TREMBLED BEFORE **VALI**, THE MIGHTY KING OF KISHKINDHA. VALI'S PARENTS WERE PROUD OF THEIR SON AND SUGREEVA, HIS BROTHER, ADORED HIM.

AT THAT TIME, THERE LIVED A RAKSHASA CALLED DUNDUBHI WHO CONSIDERED HIMSELF THE MIGHTIEST OF ALL CREATION. ONE DAY, HE WENT TO THE OCEAN, SPOILING FOR A COMBAT. BUT—

HA! HA! THE OCEAN HOLDS ME IN DREAD.

I CANNOT TAKE YOU ON. HOWEVER, I KNOW OF ONE WHO SHOULD BE ABLE TO—HIMAVAN, THE KING OF THE MOUNTAINS. GO TO HIM.

DUNDUBHI THUNDERED UP TO THE MOUNTAIN AND BREAKING OFF HUGE WHITE CLIFFS ...

... ROARED WITH GLEE, AS HE DASHED THEM TO THE PLAIN BELOW.

HIMAVAN WAS ALARMED.

WHY DO YOU TORMENT ME, THE REFUGE OF PEACE-LOVING SOULS?

IF YOU DON'T HAVE THE STRENGTH TO FIGHT ME, THEN TELL ME WHO HAS. I WILL ENTER INTO COMBAT WITH HIM.

VALI, THE MIGHTY KING OF KISHKINDHA, IS A SKILFUL WARRIOR. IN HIM YOU WILL MEET YOUR MATCH.

TRANSFORMING HIMSELF INTO A MEAN-LOOKING BUFFALO, DUNDUBHI CHARGED UP TO THE GATES OF KISHKINDHA...

GR-R-R-!

...AND BURST THEM OPEN.

GR-R-R-!

HEARING THE COMMOTION, VALI WHO WAS RELAXING WITH HIS WIVES, RUSHED OUT.

I KNOW IT IS YOU, DUNDUBHI. HOW DARE YOU BELLOW AT THE GATES OF MY CITY! IF YOU VALUE YOUR LIFE...

HOW DARE YOU SPEAK TO ME LIKE THAT IN THE PRESENCE OF WOMEN! I COME TO CHALLENGE YOU TO A COMBAT, VALI.

I AM WILLING, HOWEVER, TO GIVE YOU ONE NIGHT TO ENJOY YOUR LAST HOURS. BESIDES, YOU ARE INTOXICATED NOW AND IT IS CRIMINAL TO ATTACK A DRUNKARD. TOMORROW I SHALL KILL YOU.

WITHOUT UTTERING ANOTHER WORD, VALI SEIZED DUNDUBHI BY THE HORNS ...

...AND DASHED HIM TO THE GROUND.

BUT DUNDUBHI GOT UP CALMLY ...

... AND CHARGED.

VALI, HOWEVER, WAS READY FOR HIM WITH AN UPROOTED TREE.

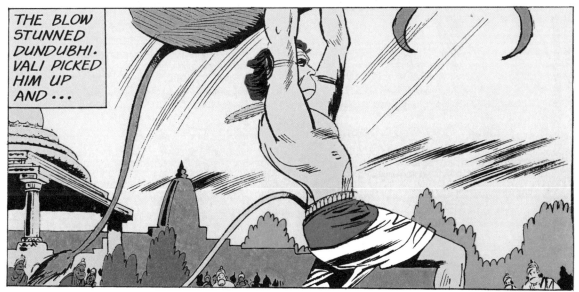

THE BLOW STUNNED DUNDUBHI. VALI PICKED HIM UP AND ...

...HURLED HIM TO THE GROUND WITH ALL HIS MIGHT.

THAT SHOULD FINISH HIM!.

WHEN THE INVINCIBLE DUNDUBHI BREATHED HIS LAST, VALI LIFTED HIS MANGLED CARCASS...

...AND FLUNG IT IN THE AIR.

UNFORTUNATELY FOR VALI, THE CARCASS FELL NEAR RISHI MATANGA'S HERMITAGE, ON THE RISHYAMUKA MOUNTAINS, FOUR MILES AWAY.

WHO DARES DESTROY THE TREES THAT I HAVE NURTURED LIKE MY OWN CHILDREN? WHO DARES DEFILE MY HERMITAGE?

BY HIS YOGIC POWER, THE RISHI DIVINED THAT VALI WAS RESPONSIBLE.

IF THAT MONKEY EVER SETS FOOT HERE, MAY HE DIE.

WHEN VALI LEARNT OF THE IRATE RISHI'S CURSE, HE CAME TO PLEAD WITH HIM.

FORGIVE ME, HOLY ONE. I DID NOT DO IT DELIBERATELY. PLEASE RELEASE ME FROM THE CURSE.

NO. I WILL NOT. YOU HAVE POLLUTED MY RETREAT. I CANNOT FORGIVE YOU.

VALI RETURNED TO KISHKINDHA. ONE DARK NIGHT, A FEW DAYS LATER —

O MIGHTY VALI, I, MAYAVI, THE SON OF DUNDUBHI, DARE YOU TO FIGHT ME.

VALI, WHO WAS SLEEPING, WOKE UP IN A RAGE.

THIS WILL BE THE LAST TIME YOU CHALLENGE ANYONE, MAYAVI.

LORD! RAKSHASAS ARE STRONGER BY NIGHT. PLEASE WAIT UNTIL DAWN TO FIGHT HIM.

BUT BRUSHING HIS WISE WIFE ASIDE, VALI STOMPED OUT.

HEARING THE COMMOTION, SUGREEVA, TOO, WOKE UP AND LOOKED QUESTIONINGLY AT TARA, VALI'S WIFE.

IT'S MAYAVI! HE'S THROWN A CHALLENGE AND THE KING HAS GONE OUT TO MEET HIM.

AT THIS HOUR? I'LL GO OUT TOO.

WHEN MAYAVI SAW VALI COME OUT, FOLLOWED CLOSELY BY SUGREEVA —

I CAN TAKE ON ONE OF THEM BUT NOT TWO!

AND MAYAVI FLED IN PANIC.

HE MUST BE TAUGHT A LESSON. I'M NOT GOING TO LET HIM ESCAPE, SUGREEVA.

I AM COMING TOO, DEAR BROTHER.

VALI AND SUGREEVA PURSUED MAYAVI THROUGH NARROW MOUNTAIN PATHS ...

...AND DENSE FORESTS.

AT LAST —

AH! THERE IS MY CAVE. ONCE INSIDE, I'M SAFE. THEY DARE NOT FOLLOW ME IN.

VALI WAS FURIOUS.

YOU WAIT HERE AND GUARD THE MOUTH OF THE CAVE, DEAR SUGREEVA.

I'M GOING AFTER HIM.

PLEASE DON'T, VALI. MAYAVI IS DANGEROUS.

I CANNOT RETURN TO THE CITY WITHOUT KILLING HIM.

AND VALI ENTERED THE HUGE CAVE SWINGING HIS MACE WILDLY...

...WHILE SUGREEVA TOOK HIS POST AT THE MOUTH OF THE CAVE.

ALAS! MY BROTHER HAS GONE TO HIS DOOM.

MANY DAYS PASSED. SUGREEVA WAS WORRIED.

WHY HASN'T VALI COME OUT? IS HE DEAD? WILL I EVER SEE HIM AGAIN?

THEN ONE DAY, ALMOST A YEAR LATER, SUGREEVA HEARD A ROAR.

GRRRR

STARTLED, HE PEEPED INTO THE CAVE.

SUDDENLY A STREAM OF BLOOD GUSHED OUT, FOLLOWED BY ANOTHER ROAR.

GRRRRR

THAT WAS MAYAVI'S CRY OF TRIUMPH. ALAS, HE HAS KILLED VALI! I WISH MY BROTHER HAD HEEDED MY WARNING.

WE ARE WITHOUT A KING. WHEN MAYAVI COMES OUT, HE WILL CERTAINLY DESTROY OUR KINGDOM. I MUST DO SOMETHING FAST.

THERE! THAT SHOULD PREVENT HIM FROM EVER COMING OUT. HE'LL DIE INSIDE.

SUGREEVA BLOCKED THE MOUTH OF THE CAVE WITH A HUGE ROCK.

INSIDE THE CAVE, HOWEVER—

THERE! I HAVE FINISHED THE SCOUNDREL. I MUST RUSH OUT! SUGREEVA MUST BE ANXIOUS.

VALI STRODE. TRIUMPHANTLY TOWARDS THE MOUTH OF THE CAVE. BUT—

THE ENTRANCE! IT'S BLOCKED! SUGREEVA HAS BETRAYED ME FOR THE THRONE!

IT WAS AN UNFAIR THOUGHT. FOR SUGREEVA WAS INNOCENT. HE HAD RETURNED TO KISHKINDHA, A VERY SAD MONKEY.

I MUST NOT TELL ANYONE ABOUT VALI'S DEATH. IT WILL CAUSE PANIC IN KISHKINDHA. I'LL KEEP QUIET.

HIS FRIEND, HANUMAN, A NOBLE AT THE COURT, APPROACHED HIM ONE DAY —

WHAT IS WRONG, O PRINCE? WHERE IS OUR KING? WHY DO YOU LOOK SO SAD?

SUGREEVA REMAINED SILENT.

THE THRONE CANNOT REMAIN VACANT. YOU MUST TAKE VALI'S PLACE.

HOW CAN I TAKE MY BROTHER'S PLACE?

BUT THE NOBLES INSISTED.

ALL RIGHT. FOR THE SAKE OF THE PEOPLE I WILL ASCEND THE THRONE.

SUGREEVA ALLOWED HIMSELF TO BE CROWNED KING. HANUMAN SERVED HIM WELL AS A MINISTER.

MEANWHILE, VALI TRIED IN VAIN TO FIND A WAY OUT OF THE CAVE. AT LAST—

I'LL KICK THE ROCK WITH ALL MY STRENGTH. IT'S BOUND TO GIVE WAY.

A FEW DAYS LATER—

IT IS VALI, OUR KING. HE IS ALIVE. HE HAS COME BACK.

O VALI, MY DEAR BROTHER. I AM HAPPY TO SEE YOU. I HAVE PRESERVED THE THRONE FOR YOU.

BUT VALI WAS IN NO MOOD FOR LOVING REUNIONS.

YOU HYPOCRITE. IT WAS YOU WHO TRAPPED ME IN THE CAVE.

VALI, I THOUGHT YOU WERE DEAD. I HEARD MAYAVI'S. ROAR. I DID NOT WANT HIM TO COME OUT AND DESTROY KISHKINDHA. THAT IS WHY I BLOCKED THE CAVE.

YOU LIE. YOU KNEW IT WAS MAYAVI'S BLOOD THAT YOU SAW, SUGREEVA. YOU KNEW IT WAS HE WHO WAS DYING.

FRIENDS, MY TREACHEROUS BROTHER BLOCKED THE CAVE SO THAT HE COULD BECOME KING. I'LL KILL HIM.

O VALI, THIS IS NOT TRUE! IT IS YOUR THRONE. PLEASE TAKE THE CROWN.

BUT VALI WAS NOT CONVINCED.

NOW LEAVE MY COUNTRY. I'LL KILL YOU, IF I SEE YOU AGAIN, SUGREEVA.

AS FOR YOUR FRIENDS, THEY WILL BE SENT TO PRISON.

HAVE MERCY ON ME, MY BROTHER. I AM INNOCENT.

BUT VALI DID NOT RELENT. SUGREEVA HAD TO LEAVE KISHKINDHA. HIS WIFE, RUMA, WAS ABOUT TO FOLLOW HIM WHEN —

NO, RUMA. YOU ARE MINE NOW AND WILL STAY WITH ME.

HANUMAN, HOWEVER, JOINED SUGREEVA AND BOTH LEFT KISHKINDHA.

LET US TAKE REFUGE NEAR RISHI MATANGA'S HERMITAGE IN THE RISHYA-MUKA MOUN-TAINS WHERE VALI DARE NOT SET FOOT.

THEY HAD TO PASS THROUGH DENSE FORESTS ...

...AND CROSS THE RIVER PAMPA BEFORE THEY COULD REACH THE RISHYAMUKA MOUNTAINS.

ONE DAY, SUGREEVA SAW TWO ARMED YOUTHS APPROACHING.

VALI MUST HAVE SENT THEM TO KILL US. FEAR FILLS MY HEART. GO AS MY ENVOY, HANUMAN. FIND OUT WHO THEY ARE.

ASSUMING THE GUISE OF A BRAHMAN, HANUMAN WITH ONE MIGHTY LEAP...

...STOOD IN THE PATH OF THE TWO STRANGERS.

WHO ARE YOU? WHAT BRINGS YOU TO THIS INACCESSIBLE FOREST?

THIS IS MY BROTHER, RAMA, THE BANISHED PRINCE OF AYODHYA. HIS WIFE SITA WAS ABDUCTED BY RAVANA, THE DEMON KING. WHO ARE YOU?

I AM HANUMAN, THE MINISTER OF SUGREEVA, KING OF THE MONKEYS. BANISHED BY HIS BROTHER, VALI, HE HAS SOUGHT REFUGE IN THESE REGIONS.

HE HAS SENT ME HERE TO TELL YOU THAT HE DESIRES YOUR FRIENDSHIP.

WE HAVE HEARD OF HIS MIGHT AND HAVE COME IN SEARCH OF HIM. INDEED WE SEEK HIS HELP TO RESCUE SITA.

HANUMAN WAS DELIGHTED.

THEN COME, I WILL TAKE YOU TO HIM.

WITH THESE VIRTUOUS, VALIANT PRINCES ON HIS SIDE, SUGREEVA CANNOT BUT REGAIN THE KINGDOM AND HIS WIFE.

THEN HANUMAN ASSUMED HIS OWN FORM AND LIFTING THE TWO BROTHERS ONTO HIS SHOULDERS...

...CARRIED THEM TO SUGREEVA.

AFTER HANUMAN HAD TOLD SUGREEVA WHO THEY WERE AND WHY THEY HAD COME —

I AM FORTUNATE THAT YOU SEEK MY FRIENDSHIP. I, TOO, NEED YOUR HELP TO KILL VALI AND WIN BACK MY WIFE.

VALI SHALL NOT ESCAPE MY ARROW.

AND WHEREVER SHE IS TO BE FOUND, I WILL FIND SITA AND BRING HER BACK TO YOU.

THEN SUGREEVA WARNED RAMA OF VALI'S STRENGTH.

I DON'T KNOW HOW YOU WILL OVERCOME HIM.

WHAT CAN RAMA DO TO CONVINCE YOU THAT HE IS EVEN STRONGER?

SUGREEVA TOLD THEM OF VALI'S ENCOUNTER WITH DUNDUBHI. THEN —

THAT IS DUNDUBHI'S SKELETON. CAN YOU, WITH A SINGLE KICK, SEND IT FLYING TWO HUNDRED BOW-LENGTHS AWAY?

RAMA EFFORTLESSLY KICKED THE SKELETON AND ⋯

...SENT IT FLYING BEYOND THE STIPULATED DISTANCE.

HOWEVER—

THAT WAS VERY GOOD, RAMA. BUT, A SKELETON IS LIGHTER. BESIDES, VALI FLUNG THE CARCASS AFTER THE FIGHT WHEN HE WAS TIRED. HOW DO I JUDGE WHO IS STRONGER?

AND HOW SHALL I CONVINCE YOU THAT I CAN DEFEAT VALI?

DO YOU SEE THOSE SAL TREES? VALI EFFORTLESSLY PIERCED SEVEN OF THEM, ONE AFTER THE OTHER, WITH HIS ARROWS.

IF YOU CAN PIERCE ALL OF THEM WITH ONE ARROW, I WILL BE CONVINCED THAT YOU ARE MORE POWERFUL THAN HIM.

IS THAT ALL?

RAMA LIFTED HIS BOW AND AIMED AT THE FIRST OF THE SEVEN TREES.

THE ARROW PIERCED ALL THE SEVEN TREES...

...AND RETURNED TO RAMA'S QUIVER.

I AM CONVINCED THAT YOU ARE STRONGER.

COME, SUGREEVA. LET US GO TO KISHKINDHA IMMEDIATELY. YOU GO AHEAD OF US AND CHALLENGE VALI.

AT KISHKINDHA, RAMA AND LAXMANA HID ON THE BRANCHES OF A TREE WHILE SUGREEVA CHALLENGED VALI.

WHERE ARE YOU, YOU COWARDLY USURPER?I HAVE COME TO WREST THE THRONE FROM YOU.

BURNING WITH RAGE, VALI RUSHED OUT TO CONFRONT HIS BROTHER.

SUGREEVA'S STRENGTH, HOWEVER, SOON WANED AND HE KEPT LOOKING BACK.

WHEN IS RAMA GOING TO HELP?

SUDDENLY, SUGREEVA RAN TOWARDS HIS MOUNTAIN HIDEOUT.

RAMA HAS LET ME DOWN. I'D BETTER ESCAPE WHILE I STILL HAVE THE STRENGTH.

VALI PURSUED HIM. BUT SUGREEVA ENTERED SAGE MATANGA'S HERMITAGE.

THE COWARD! HE KNOWS I DARE NOT FOLLOW HIM THERE.

LATER, CHOKING WITH EMOTION, SUGREEVA, REPROACHED RAMA.

WHY DID YOU ASK ME TO CHALLENGE VALI WHEN YOU HAD NO INTENTION OF HELPING ME? WHY DID YOU LET HIM DEFEAT ME?

MY FRIEND, HAVE FAITH. I JUST COULD NOT DISTINGUISH YOU FROM YOUR BROTHER. I DID NOT WANT TO KILL YOU, EVEN BY MISTAKE.

RAMA ASKED SUGREEVA TO CHALLENGE VALI AGAIN.

WEAR THIS GARLAND AROUND YOUR NECK AND FIGHT. AND VALI WILL NOT RETURN ALIVE.

SUGREEVA ONCE AGAIN CONFRONTED VALI.

O VALI, THIS TIME I'LL KILL YOU. COME OUT AND FIGHT.

WHEN VALI HEARD HIS ROAR—

IT'S THAT TRAITOR AGAIN. THIS TIME I'LL KILL HIM.

27

AS VALI WAS ABOUT TO LEAVE THE PALACE TO MEET SUGREEVA—

MY LORD, OUR SPIES TELL ME THAT SUGREEVA HAS TWO FRIENDS FROM AYODHYA ON HIS SIDE.

MY SWEET ONE, DO NOT WORRY. I KNOW WHO THEY ARE. I KNOW THEY WILL NOT INTERFERE.

HE IS AFTER ALL YOUR BROTHER. WHY DON'T YOU MAKE PEACE WITH HIM?

I CANNOT. I MUST TEACH HIM A LESSON. BUT I WILL NOT KILL HIM.

AND VALI ADVANCED TOWARDS SUGREEVA.

THIS TIME I'LL BREAK EVERY BONE IN YOUR BODY.

A FURIOUS FIGHT TOOK PLACE BETWEEN THE TWO BROTHERS.

SUDDENLY, SUGREEVA RAISED HIS HANDS.

THERE'S HIS SIGNAL.

AND RAMA TOOK AIM.

THE ARROW FOUND ITS MARK. VALI FELL.

LATER, WHEN RAMA APPROACHED HIM WITH LAXMANA AND THE OTHERS—

O RAMA, WHAT RIGHT DID YOU HAVE TO KILL ME— I, WHO HAD FULL FAITH IN YOUR VIRTUE AND WISDOM? I HAVE DONE YOU NO HARM.

I KNOW YOU CAME TO SUGREEVA FOR HELP. IF YOU HAD ONLY ASKED ME ONCE, I WOULD HAVE CAPTURED RAVANA AND BROUGHT HIM TO YOU. OH, WHY DID YOU INTERFERE IN OUR FIGHT?

IT IS THE DUTY OF A KING TO METE OUT JUSTICE—TO PROTECT THE OPPRESSED AND PUNISH THE OPPRESSOR. YOU HAVE WRONGED YOUR YOUNGER BROTHER WHOM YOU SHOULD HAVE CHERISHED AS YOUR SON. YOU DESERVE TO DIE.

VALI WAS FULL OF REMORSE WHEN HE HEARD THOSE WORDS.

I CANNOT BUT ADMIT THAT WHAT YOU SAY IS TRUE. PLEASE FORGIVE ME, RAMA. DO NOT VISIT MY SINS UPON MY BELOVED SON, ANGADA, OR HIS WISE MOTHER, TARA.

DO NOT WORRY, VALI. SUGREEVA AND I SHALL LOVE ANGADA AS YOU LOVED HIM.

MEANWHILE, TARA, VALI'S WIFE, AND ANGADA, HIS SON, CAME ON THE SCENE.

MY LORD! O KING! WHY DIDN'T YOU HEED MY WORDS? WHAT AM I TO DO NOW? WHAT WILL THE ANGRY SUGREEVA, WHO HATES US, DO TO ANGADA?

SUGREEVA AND RAMA WILL CARE FOR YOU AND ANGADA, AS I DID.

SUGREEVA, MY HOUR HAS COME. PLEASE FORGIVE ME. I DID NOT KNOW WHAT I WAS DOING.

O VALI, IT WAS YOUR LOVE I ALWAYS WANTED, NOT THE THRONE. YOU NEVER UNDERSTOOD.

DO NOT GRIEVE, SUGREEVA. TAKE THIS GOLDEN CHAIN. MAY IT BRING YOU SUCCESS. PLEASE RULE KISHKINDHA PROPERLY, O SUGREEVA. TAKE CARE OF MY WIFE AND SON.

AND VALI BREATHED HIS LAST, HAVING SETTLED ALL WORLDLY MATTERS IN A MANNER BEFITTING A KING.

# CELEBRATING
## 50
### AMAR CHITRA KATHA
#### YEARS

It was in 1967 that the first Amar Chitra Katha comic rolled off the presses, changing story-telling for children across India forever.

Five decades and more than 400 books later, we are still sharing stories from India's rich heritage, primarily because of the love and support shown by readers like yourself.

## SO, FROM US TO YOU, HERE'S A BIG
# THANK YOU!